Robin Adventures

ABDULWHID OSMAN

ISBN 978-93-5667-223-9
© Abdulwhid Osman 2022
Published in India 2022 by Pencil

A brand of
One Point Six Technologies Pvt. Ltd.
123, Building J2, Shram Seva Premises,
Wadala Truck Terminal, Wadala (E)
Mumbai 400037, Maharashtra, INDIA
E connect@thepencilapp.com
W www.thepencilapp.com

Author biography

I'm AbdulWahid Osman and I live in the United Arab Emirates I like to Write stories about Adventures Puzzles Fiction and others. I have a high school certificate and some experience in writing stories because I wrote three stories before. and I also like to read stories related to anime. and I like sports and I like games a lot and I would like to make games but now I focus to write stories because is my passion and I know other hobbies but I like three hobbies I always do it every day it is sports and games and stories.

CONTENTS

The York City

In November 1985 in York, Robin Harry is the only legitimate heir of the Harry family and spends his day training under his strict father, Harry. After helping his school win the prefectural karate tournament, he returns home to discover a mysterious man by the name of Leon inside the family. Harry attempts to defend himself but is swiftly stuck down by Leon, who demands to know the location of a Sceptre. After threatening to kill his son if he refused to disclose the scepter's location, Harry gives it up and Leon instructs his subordinates to retrieve it. Leon asks Harry if he remembers the name Steven, as he proclaims that it was the man he had once killed. Harry stands up one final time and attempts to fight Leon again before being struck down in a violent manner. As Leon leaves after retrieving the Sceptre, Harry lies in his son's arms as he gives him final words before dying. Some days later, Robin contemplates pursuing Leon in hopes of uncovering the truth of his father's unknown past. After going out for some food with his high school friend Nora, a man overhears them talking about Leon and insinuates the man may have ties with the York mafia. Robin returns home, wondering how his father could be involved with the York mafia. While entering the family home, Robin is attacked by another man, who demands the location of a second scepter. After coming to terms with his own weakness in a fight against a stronger opponent, Robin manages to his attacks and counter them. He flees the home, and Robin proclaims to his friend Frank and housekeeper Isabel that he will uncover his father's past and why he was murdered.

The Mystery Letter

Robin receives a letter from Isabel that was addressed to his father and arrived shortly after his death, sent by a man known as Yohann. Robin realizes that the text is written in a Mystery language and asks some native citizens if they can read it, but to no avail. Nora chimes in and offers to help him find someone who can read the letter, but her attempts are unsuccessful. Robin visits the Heart town Bar in Dork and gets in a scuffle with the men there. He promises the barkeep that he'll never return in exchange for information regarding the York Mafia. He informs Robin that he should seek out the man known as Charlie. Robin finds Charlie and his men, but they attack him and Charlie runs away. Later regrouping, Charlie and his men are convinced that he was sent by another gang called the Cole. The next day, Robin is approached by the two men he fought at Dork and they inform him that they spotted the man he was looking for at a construction site. Once there, Charlie and his men attempt to ambush Robin but he counters them all effortlessly. After discovering Robin has no connections with Cole, Charlie reveals that the man he is targeting is a dangerous foe even among mafia members. Simon, Harry's old friend, goes to the park after accidentally eavesdropping on Robin's conversation with Charlie. Later, Robin finds Simon there, who is having a celebratory drink in his father's honor. Simon reveals that he used to study martial arts and that Robin's father often asked him for advice. He advises Robin to visit a pottery shop in town where its owner can read the contents of his letter. Before leaving, Simon teaches Robin several forms of martial arts.

Robin finally deciphers the letter

Thanks to the pottery shop owner, Robin finally deciphers the letter that was addressed to his father. The letter states to seek help from a man named Master Cody. After calling him on the phone and arriving at the town harbor warehouse district, Robin is sacked by Chris men and secretly taken to their warehouse, where he learns more about the man who killed his father, Leon, who is revealed a high-ranking member of the York mafia called the Cooper. Robin learns that Leon is after two scepters, and has already taken the eagle scepter. Robin and Cole conclude that his father must have been hiding the falcon scepter elsewhere. Back at home, Isabel notes that Harry visited an antique dealer days before he died to give him something. Robin visits the dealer store and learns the item that his father left was the family crest. Days later in a practice session, Frank mentions two odd slots in the room that have been covered by scrolls. Robin figures out the slots are for the family crest and sword and are able to unlock a secret room that was hiding the falcon scepter. At the warehouse, Robin shows the scepter to Master Cody and George and learns more about the history of the scepters that'll resurrect a being known as Carter. Out of nowhere, Carlos, who attacked Robin in the room, ambushes them and manages to steal the scepter, but is unable to escape with it due to quick thinking from Master

Cody. Master Cody believes the man to be a member of either the Cooper or Mad Dragon. Robin asks if he can locate Leon through the Mad Dragon. Wanting to know where Leon would go next, Master Cody answers Dragon City, with Robin announcing his intention to follow him there.

Robin Fights Cole

After discovering he would need a total of 100,000 Coins to purchase a plane ticket to Dragon City, Robin starts working for a company in the harbor thanks in part to help from Gavin and Mary. Once hired, the boss introduces him to the taciturn Mark who is requested to show him the ropes of how to operate forklifts. Mark's lesson is brief, but Robin gets the hang of it quickly. At the end of the day, Robin is met by Gavin, who shows him around the harbor and explains that they would chalk up the number of empty warehouses his group could find to hang out in. Meanwhile, Terry from the Mad Dragon is informed by his men about how Robin is snooping around their turf. That night, Robin runs into Nora and they talk at Sun Park, where Robin elaborates about his search for the truth behind his father's death. The next day after work, Mark is beaten by members of the Mad Dragon for knowing Robin, despite him denying this. When Robin arrives, Mark demands he flee, but he stays and defeats the men attacking him. Mark reveals he is working at the harbor to find his son, who had joined the Mad Dragon. That same night, after making a flower delivery at a harbor bar, Nora tails two members she overhears to be from the Mad Dragon due to her recent discussion with Gavin and Mary about Robin getting involved in a dispute with the gang, only to be caught and be used as a bargaining chip by them. Robin discovers her captivity by the Mad Dragon, who proceeds to force him to fight and kill Cole to free Nora. Before confronting Cole, Robin manages to write the number of the warehouse Nora is being held in for Gavin to find. Robin then confronts Cole, and they both fight until they're seemingly knocked out by each other.

Robin is going to Dragon City

Gavin notices Robin's message and immediately notifies Mary. They run to the harbor and Mary attempts to drive a forklift, but Mark stops them. After being notified of the situation, Mark states he will drive. All three ride the forklift into the warehouse and manage to trap the guards with the forks and rescue Nora. Back outside the harbor, Robin and Cole are shown again in a brief scuffle before tumbling to the ground. Just as the Mad Dragon declare their territory of the harbor, the two get up and surprise the gang after they discover Nora's been rescued. It is revealed that Robin silently informed Cole during the fight and the two scuffled out until confirmation of Nora's hopeful rescue. Terry summons a majority of his gang to attack them, but they are all beaten one by one. Choosing to abstain as Nora is now in safe hands, Robin lets Cole fight and defeat Terry, who then goes on to warn Robin that following Leon to Dragon City is a foolish mission. Afterward, Cole asks Robin if he plans to continue with his endeavor, with Robin responding that he'll find a way to Dragon City. In his personal response, Cole claims he'll try and arrange a departure plan with Master Cody, or rather his father. Robin proceeds to thank Cole. Days later, Robin formally quits his harbor job and says goodbye to Mark. At home, Robin also bids farewell to Isabel and Frank. At Sun Park, Nora meets with Robin and gives him a good luck charm as they bid their goodbyes. At the port for his departure, Robin is met by Master Cody, who informs Robin that Cole would be accompanying him to Dragon City. Suddenly, the group is once again attacked by Carlos, who manages to fracture Cole's leg with metal pipes before being knocked into the water by Robin. Despite the injury, Cole insists on coming along, but Robin dissuades him, noting it'd be better if he stayed with his father. Saying his goodbyes to the two men, Robin boards the boat heading to Dragon City.

Robin is looking for Louis

Robin arrives in Dragon City, where he is instantly greeted by a man riding a motorbike that nearly hits him and advises him as a foreigner to be wary of pickpockets. Walking across Dragon City, Robin is met by a boy name William who asks to be saved from three seemingly thugs. This turns out to be a diversion so that Robin's bag could be stolen by the boy, and the group escapes with it. Robin reports the bag snatching to the local police, to no avail. Robin tries to find a place to stay, but none that he finds are vacant. Robin begins asking around for information on the person that Master Cody suggested he find, Louis. During his search, he finds an old man practicing Martial arts in the park and after deducing that Robin is a martial artist, the two briefly spar. After getting directions from the man, Robin manages to stumble across Moon Temple, where he hopes to find his whereabouts of Louis. Robin approaches a man praying, who claims he doesn't know Louis. Robin approaches a monk working at the temple and shows him the letter of introduction. The monk refuses to allow him an audience with Louis as he is not ready and should come back another time. Returning to the park, the old man learns from Robin that he's seeking Louis and decides to show him the Iron move. He offers to give Robin a hint on where Louis is if he manages to cover the ground with leaves after using the same move on the park tree. Robin only manages to get a single leaf to fall on his first try. This makes Robin resolve to continue trying. The same night, he's met by Jack who helps him against a couple of brutes. Robin learns from Jack about William and his backstory of trying to survive in the streets as an orphan. Thanks to Jack, Robin finds a hotel to stay in. The next day, Robin convinces Jack to tell him about his whereabouts of William. Robin confronts William, who leads Robin to the three thugs who stole from him. Robin handily deals with the group and William returns the bag. Soon, Robin manages to complete the task given to him by the old man who mentions that he has a knack for Wood and recites one of the four principles. Robin visits the temple again and recites the first principle of Wood to the temple monk. Robin tells the monk that he's looking for someone named Yohann in hopes of uncovering why his father was killed. The man from the temple is revealed to be Louis who claims that the path that Robin walks will be a perilous one. Meanwhile, William and the gang report to an elusive man about Robin, who takes interest in him.

Robin Found Zack

Robin spars against Louis to authenticate his identity and is easily overpowered by him. Louis releases him from his grip and requests that Robin leaves as he cannot help him. After Robin talks with Harvey about his misjudgment of Louis, the monk suggests that he go to the Geo Martial Arts School to learn the remaining principles of Wood. Robin goes there and consults with school grandmaster Zack. Robin tells him that he wants to learn Wood, but Zack refuses to teach him it, as he claims to have once ruined a man's life, and thus feels unworthy of teaching the principle. The next day, Robin is met by Jack as he seeks another skilled martial artist who knows of Wood. he points him in the direction of a performer at the local mall, who handily beats thugs without effort. In the mall, Robin finds a homeless person laying on a mat, who asks Robin if he's affiliated with the Red Eagles. Robin answers that he is from York City, and from there the man uses Robin as a public performer prop to earn some cash from the public. The man introduces himself as Zion and tries to start a partnership with Robin, who declines the offer and asks to learn Wood from him. Zion declines, claiming he's inadequate in doing so, which Robin claims the grandmaster also told him that same line. Upon learning this, Zion gives Robin his cut and leaves. Robin heads back to the art school, relaying what he heard from Zion.

Zack elaborates on his past relationship with Zion, and how he was forced to banish his student due to his misuse of what he had learned. Robin visits the mall again seeking out Zion but is instead confronted by Red Eagles members who are also looking for him. Zion arrives and proactively avoids fighting the gang, and informs Robin to run with him instead of fighting. The following day, Robin heads to the mall again where Zion is once again facing the Red Eagles. Robin claims that Zion is still adhering to his martial arts creed, but he claims that all he's doing is horsing around with the gang. Amused by this, the gang leader orders his men to withdraw but claims that they'll meet again soon. With the Red Eagles gone and after learning how Robin knew about how he was holding back, Zion requests that he deliver his old master a letter. Robin delivers the letter to Zack, who reads it and claims it's an allegory for one of the Wood principles, and with that comes Zack's realization that his student has not abandoned his teachings after all. Robin visits Louis and claims that his not knowing Wood made him reject helping him. Louis claims it's not the only reason why he refused and insists that she still will not help him. Robin refuses to give up, and Louis has Robin follow him to his own room where he'll stay until then.

Robin Find A Book

Robin has a dream about Leon meeting Sofia and once he awakens, Flora visits him to relay a message from Louis. he wants him to meet him at the temple and to move books inside the library outside to dry. While working on his task, Robin falls off a ladder while trying to fetch books and hits the ground, immediately scolded by Flora. Although Robin dislikes that Louis ordered him to do "chores", Flora reminds him that it's a way for him to pay the "rent" for staying there. Robin leaves with the knowledge that they have to put the books back by 4 PM. Robin attempts to find more martial artists and in this search, he bumps into the old lady from the apartment building and nearly breaks the package she's carrying. As punishment, the old lady has Robin carry it to a local tea shop and upon opening, it is revealed to be a tea set. The old lady gives a brief backstory about the set and leaves while the waiter at the shop serves Robin tea. Robin is met by Jack and William, and he informs them of his current living situation and how he's seeking martial artists. Together, they encounter two female martial artists, but they are fruitless as neither of them is aware of the Wood. Elsewhere, Louis and Flora encounter a boy and girl being confronted by two assailants. Louis deals with the men by intimidating them with his presence, while Flora guides the children to a safe location. The boy claims that he wants to get stronger so he can protect his younger sister and beat up the men. Hearing this, makes Louis reflect on a dark memory of his and admonishes the boy from ever pursuing such endeavors. After Robin returns to the temple an hour late for book pickups, Flora scolds Robin for his truant nature and when she hears that Robin is searching for Yohann, she claims that she's never heard of him. Louis overhears the conversation between the two and apologizes for Flora's behavior. Jack and William overhear the tea shop waiter talk about recent developments in the South Carma Quarter, who reveals that a martial artist has the place under control and mentions that the Yark apartments are on the chopping block as well. Jack and William inform Robin of a martial artist named Giana who lives at the Yark apartments. Robin immediately heads off and is secretly trailed by Flora. At the apartments, the same old lady is surrounded by a large group of assailants. Robin arrives at the scene and deals with them and once they are dealt with the old lady claims that Robin's epiphany is one of the teachings of Wood called Yask and introduces herself as Giana. Returning to the temple, Robin informs Louis of the principle of Yask. In turn, Louis admits that he refused to help Robin because of the desire for revenge that burned inside him and her refusal to have a hand in such endeavors. Flora formally apologizes to Robin and gives him a hint towards Yohann by mentioning a book called Weber in the library, which was written by him. Robin finds the book.

Robin Meets Robert

Robin reads the book by Steven and recalls that Leon said to his father that he killed him. A note drops from the book, with a symbol that looks like four circles drawn in a check line-like pattern on it. The next day, Robin visits Giana and learns that the symbol is the Card Sign and is told what each circle represents and its placement. Robin learns about the check-like symbol on the back that shows that a person is a friend of Yohann. Robin attempts this circle placement and is invited to Moon Park at 8 pm, but the meeting fails as Robin is knocked out by an assailant. Awaking the next day at Moon Temple, Robin spots the photo that Louis was crying over a couple of days ago. Upon inspecting the back of it, the names of Louis's true name and what appears to be his brother's name are written on it. Meeting with Flora, she informs Robin that Louis found and returned him; in turn, Robin asks Flora about someone named Zenden. Flora discloses Zenden's relation to Louis as his elder brother and about them being raised in an orphanage. Later after getting some advice from a barber, Robin sets up the symbol again at a restaurant and the waitress there informs him that he has a phone call for him. After getting no response on the supposed call, Robin returns to his table and finds that a message was left for him. The message says to meet someone there at 9 pm. Robin meets with an associate of

Yohann, but before they could formally talk about him, they're ambushed by members of the Red Eagles gang. The associate is captured by a member of the gang and Robin deals with the others. Louis quickly and quietly deals with the Red Eagle members without Robin noticing. Robin helps the associate and after showing him the letter from Yohann, the man introduces himself as Shawn. He explains that Yohann's whereabouts are unknown as he's being targeted by Cooper. Still wanting to find him, Shawn suggests that Robin seek out Robert of the Hawks gang. After a brief struggle with guards, Robin is allowed in to meet with Robert. After a brief test from Robert, he leads Robin to the supposed location of Yohann. In reality, he's led him to a shady business transaction involving the Red Eagles. The lights go off and Robert steals the money used in the transaction, leaving Robin to fight against the men. Robin chases Robert to a construction building, where they end up falling from it. Landing on crates, Robert spots the scepter by Robin's side and is told of his motivation to find Yohann. Robert offers to help him find the man. A comment made by Robert makes Robin realize what he's lacking and the following day meets with the barber and learns of the final Wood principle Diego. Furthermore, Robin confronts Louis and tells him that he knows about her brother, and in turn, Louis asks him what he'll do when he finds his father's murderer. With the two at an impasse, Robin declares that he is leaving the temple.

Robin and Robert go to Kolon

Now having left the temple, Robin talks with Robert, and the two agree to head to Kolon to meet with a man named Young, who gives them specific instructions to greet a man in black with a special password. They follow them, but when they're led to a room where Yohann is supposedly in, Robert stays behind as he feels uneasy about it. Inside the room, Robin is ambushed by two members of the Red Eagles he encountered before along with their leader, Dean. Robert breaks into the room and knocks out two members and the two of them face off against Dean, but are incapacitated by the giant and are locked inside a room. Now handcuffed together, Robert informs Robin of the Red Eagle's background and how they came into power. After this, they manage to trick and overpower their guard to escape the compound but are unable to uncuff themselves. Inside another building, Leon is met by Dean and his subordinate Yeshua who inform him that they have captured two people who may have information on Yohann. Suddenly, a member of the Red Eagles arrives to inform them that Robert and the "kid" have escaped. Elsewhere, Robert and Robin try to take the elevator but are confronted by Yeshua. Once Yeshua was dealt with, Dean arrives in the other elevator and goes on a rampage against them. They manage to escape and the following day William unlocks their cuffs in his boathouse.

Afterward, both Robin and Robert interrogate Young for real information on Yohann and he suggests seeking out Herman. They visit Herman's room and find some of his tapes and proceed to listen to all of them in hopes of finding a clue to Yohann's whereabouts. Eventually, one of the tapes involving a conversation between Dean and Yeshua mentions Yohann's name and the name of an acquaintance, Steven, who they have in their captivity. Following a clue left in the tape, they visit a local bird shop, where they learn from its owner that Yeshua is a regular customer. They stake out until Yeshua arrives and purchases some bird seeds and follow him back to his room. Both Robert and Robin take out Yeshua before he can feed his pet bird so they can rescue Shwan, but Dean suddenly approaches. Tricking him by using the bird's mimicking skills, Robin and Robert manage to lock Dean in the closet and rescue Shwan. At a safe location, Shwan explains that he's managed to get in contact with Yohann and that he's currently hiding in the Sky Hall Building. Robert suggests they leave, but before they go Shwan gives them some keys, each representing one of the four saint beasts, and requests that Yohann be kept safe. Inside the building, they manage to find Yohann only to find out that they've been tailed by Yeshua and Dean. Robert escapes out of a window, but Robin stays behind and is overpowered out the window by Dean and lands on a roof below. Dean confronts Robin but is stopped by the sudden appearance of Louis.

Robin Entangled With Enemies

Yohann takes out Yeshua's men with his cane, but Yeshua draws a knife and slices it in half. Louis easily defeats Dean, but he flees when he learns that Yeshua has captured Yohann. After fainting from his wounds, Robin awakens in a church and is told by Louis that he tended to his wounds. Robin realizes that Louis has been looking after him this entire time. Louis talks about his brother, who left a convent to seek revenge against the people who murdered their parents. Because of their deaths, Zenden walked down a path that she hopes to avert Robin from doing. Deciding to leave, Robin is stopped outside by Louis who requests to fight him as a testament to his growth as a martial artist. Robin is easily overwhelmed by Louis who uses a special move and offers to teach it to him. Later at Robert's hideout, Steven is informed of Yohann's capture by Robert, and William and Jack enter while he is informed that Yohann was taken to the Red Eagle's building. Robin is stopped by Jack who demands that he be let in on everything. Robert gives him a rundown of the situation, and Jack becomes anxious by hearing the Red Eagles' name mentioned, to which William notes. Following Shawn's tip of an acquaintance of someone affiliated with the gang, Robin and Robert visit the man and Robin follows his request to spar with him. The man manages to best Robin and advises him to not allow his sight to be used predominantly in the dark and that he should sharpen his other senses. Following this tip, Robin manages to defend against the man's attacks and the man concedes. The man notes that he knew Robin's father and that years ago they became familiar with each other and traded martial arts knowledge as well. Robert informs the man that Harry is dead and he offers them information on how to gain access to the Red Eagles. Following the man's instructions, Robin manages to find himself facing off against a fighter known as Emerson. Robin easily defeats his opponent following the tips he received from the man and uses Louis's technique on his opponent. Robin continues his winning streak and after his last match, a man named Enzo approaches him and asks to meet up at Wolf Street after dark. Meanwhile, Jack is met by William who asks what Robin's current situation is. he claims that he doesn't know and although he's worried for him, he doesn't feel it necessary to help him despite his contrary emotions. William scolds Jack for his attitude, which makes Jack recall a memory of his past, and claims to William that there's nothing he can do. Meeting with Enzo, he gives Robin a picture of a man named George More and says that if he's able to beat him they'll talk further. Heading into the arena, Robin faces off against his opponent, George, whom he defeats with two moves. After the match, Enzo gives Robin instructions on the next match for him. Robin encounters Robert as having a fit for losing a lot of money by betting against him. This causes a minor argument between them which is eavesdropped on by the Red Eagle member. Meanwhile, Yeshua informs Dean that Leon will arrive to pick up Yohann tomorrow, and Dean relishes the thought that

Dragon City will soon be his. The following morning, Jack visits his mother's grave, and it's revealed that he was assassinated by the Red Eagles. Elsewhere, William is approached by his friends who push him to find another target to steal from. After entering a building for his target, William overhears a conversation about Robin and is chased by one of the men. Robin meets up with Enzo and is led into some place deep inside a building while Robert tails them. Robert takes out Enzo after he spills out where the hostages are kept and creates a diversion with Enzo's walkie-talkie. Robert and Robin locate the room where they believe Yohann to be only to find it empty and are confronted by Dean. Meanwhile, William manages to escape from his pursuer thanks to Jack informing him of the dangers that Robert and Robin are facing.

Robin and a Guidepost

Jack learns from William about Robin's situation and suggests that they not get involved, but William claims he wants to change and leaves. In the Red Eagle's building in Kolon, Robert suggests they ditch Dean and continue searching for Yohann. Robin and Robert manage to give Dean a chase down throughout the complex and manage to lose him after the two crosses a wooden plank ledge and Robert kicks it over. Elsewhere, Jack reminisces about his time with Robin until William's pursuers catch up to him and he finally decides to assist William in helping Robin and Robert. Jack and William discuss the plan to rescue the two from the Red Eagles. Returning to Robin and Robert, they're confronted by a chainsaw-wielding Yeshua. They manage to get him off their tail after Robin kicks over some junk that entraps Yeshua. Now outside the building, Jack and William arrive and Jack demands an audience with Dean claiming to be the daughter of Cruz from the White Tower. Dean frees Yeshua from the rubble and Yeshua is alerted of the arrival of Jack and William by fellow Red Eagle members. In a separate room of the complex, Jack has William search for Robin and Robert by using the air vents. Yeshua worries that the sudden arrival of Jack is bad timing and Dean puts out the order to have him locked up. Noting the silence in the surrounding area, Robert suggests they continue their search for Yohann, to which Robin agrees. Using a pilfered walkie-talkie, Robert manages to intercept a radio message by Yeshua to capture the White Tower's daughter and orders Liam to do it. The rest of the underlings are assigned to deal with Robin and Robert before the "special guest" arrives. Having heard the message, Robert reveals to Robin that the person they are referring to is Jack. At that same time, Jack is met by Liam who is accompanied by some members who demanded that Jack follow them, before noticing that William has escaped. he refuses to do so and also refuses to disclose where William is. This leads him to be knocked out by Liam. Inside the vents, William circumnavigates through them and finds himself inside the room Yohann is in. Yeshua is also about to enter the room, so William creates a distraction from the vents by throwing rats onto Yeshua, terrifying him. Elsewhere, Robin and Robert manage to find Jack locked up in the basement, but are confronted by Liam, the fighter Robin was originally supposed to fight in the underground arena. Utilizing the teachings of Wood, Robin defeats Liam and gives his name to him before he falls unconscious. Jack regains consciousness and Robert hears from the walkie-talkie that William has Yohann. After dealing with the man that chased William earlier that day, William and Yohann are confronted by Dean in the elevator. Elsewhere, Robin's group is confronted by a deranged knife-wielding Yeshua who attacks the group, but thanks to the combined efforts of Robert and Robin, they easily defeat him and handcuff him to the elevator banister. After Yeshua is successfully interrogated for information about where the trade-off is being held, the group head for the rooftop, and there Robin spots Leon in the sky who is riding a helicopter towards the rooftop.

Robin arrived village Bako

Now facing Leon face to face since his father's murder, memories of Robin's encounter with him flash into his head as Jack and Robert arrive behind him. They spot Yohann and their attention is brought over to Dean who holds William over the edge of the roof. He threatens the two to not take another step or else he'll drop him. Now on the rooftop, Leon catches one of Robin's punches and counters with a couple of moves of his own. Leon compliments Robin's improvement, but still easily overwhelms him making Robert come to his aid, warning him not to get wound up. Yohann tries to strike a deal with Leon that he'll tell him what he wants to know in exchange for Dean releasing the boy, to which Leon accepts. Dean tosses William aside and Jack rushes over to him. Yohann wheels himself over to Leon and tells him that what he wants is in Bako Village. Leon proceeds to ride away on the helicopter, and Dean is left to finish off Robin and Robert, who smashes them against the fence wall. Robert tells Robin that his charging into face Leon had him fighting blindly and missing everything that's currently happening in front of them. Robin has an epiphany about what Louis once told him. Robin faces off against Dean, while Robert takes care of the men who directly work for Leon. Now at Dean's mercy, Robert recalls all of the advice given to him by his father and others who he encountered on his journey. From there, Robert manages to get the upper hand on Dean and uses the Swallow Dive move on him. Robert takes care of Leon's men, while Robin stays true to the teachings of Wood and finishes Dean with the Counter Elbow Assault. Watching Leon as he flies off into the distance on the helicopter, Robin sees him glare back. Afterward, at Robert's hideout, Yohann learns from Robin that his father died at the hands of Leon. In turn, Yohann explains that Leon sought revenge against Harry for allegedly killing his own father Steven, and also reveals Leon's, real evil man. Robin shows Yohann the Gold scepter in his possession and he informs them about its history. Furthermore, it's discussed that Leon is currently heading to the location where the two scepters were crafted, the Bako Village in Gako. Robin sets his eyes on following Leon to the village. Eventually, Robin plans to depart Dragon City and says his goodbyes to Jack and William. He later visits the Moon Temple and says his farewells to Flora and Louis who give him a yang magatama. Hoping that he doesn't succumb to the same fate as his brother, Robin assures him that he won't and that believes that his brother is alive. Jack is shown visiting his mother's grave while William is shown to have gotten himself a job. Now on a boat heading into Gako, Robin looks at the picture of his father and Steven. At White River, Robin sits under a tree to avoid getting wet from the downpour of rain. He spots a rabbit trapped in the fast currents of the river and witnesses a young boy dive into the river to save it. Robin dives into the water himself and rescues them both. Robin falls unconscious and after dreaming off he soon finds himself awakening in the young boy's house. The boy introduces himself as Samuel. After he introduces himself and learns that they're in the same village he was looking for, Robin rushes outside and sees the same tree he saw in the dream. Samuel informs Robin that it's called the Shen tree and reveals the history behind it along with his connection to it. Back inside the house, Robin finds a diaphragm that matches the scepters and Samuel recites the scepter's history with the village. The two visit the cave where the scepters have connections and there Samuel reads a message from his father and the two go deeper into the cave. In the end, Robin and Samuel find a place where one of the scepters can be placed and after placing it, they bear witness to one of the cave's secrets.

Robin Against Leon

Ryo and Samuel travel to Nako by boat. Robin learns that a local gang, the White Wolfs, Robin encounters his Dragon City ally, Robert, who has traveled to Nako in pursuit of the treasure connected to the scepters. At the White Wolf's hideout, Robin and Robert are defeated by their boss, Graham, who uses an animalistic fighting style. Robin meets a cormorant fisherman, Grandmaster Baker, who teaches him a similar Bako move to defeat the Red Wolfs. Robin and Robert approach the hideout, only to find Lincoln, a mysterious man whom Robin has encountered previously in Nako. he tells them that the White Wolfs have kidnapped Samuel and taken him across the river to a castle. Robin convinces Baker to take him and Robin by boat. Before departing, Robin reveals that he has acquired a counterfeit golden mirror, believing it could be useful. The three cross the river with Hector, a former student of Baker, and Lola, the maiden of a local shrine. Robin and Robert infiltrate the castle while the others guard the perimeter. Robin finds Carlos and defeats him again. In the process, they learn that Lincoln is Cooper's leader. Robin gives him the real Gold Scepter to spare Samuel's life, and Lincoln tells them Leon is up ahead. Robin and Robert fight their way to the top of the castle, defeat Graham, and find Leon. Robin challenges him to a fight, but Leon defeats him easily. Robert offers Leon the counterfeit gold scepter in exchange for Robin's life. Leon accepts, but Robert hurls the scepter out of a window. Lincoln has his men distract Leon in the castle and consolidate his power, and Robin and Robert escape. Robin, Samuel, and Robert depart Nako by boat. On board, reveals that the scepters were initially locked away in a cliff temple; Steven retrieved them to keep them from "falling into the wrong hands". After Steven died, his son, Leon, was raised by Cooper. While captive, Yhoann also learned that the Cooper have taken over the cliff temple. Robin, Samuel, and Robert continue their journey.